The HANOVER BLOCK

THE HANOVER BLOCK

GREGOR XANE

new dollar pulp
ohio

This work is a work of fiction. All characters and events portrayed in this book are fictitious, and any resemblance to real people or events is purely coincidental.

THE HANOVER BLOCK

A New Dollar Pulp Book

Published by New Dollar Pulp

russcam75@gmail.com / russcameron.deviantart.com

Cover Design By:

the NERDGENCY

thenerdgency.com

For the exceptional Robbie Zameika

acknowledgements

I must thank the following humans (and human-like entities) for helping me to improve this piece and for suffering through its earlier incarnations: Butterfly Pingo, Ruben Boyajian, Mickey of the Fuzzy Dews, Jason Parent, Amber Foxx, and the man-beast now known as Edward Lorn.

I'd also like to thank John Overwine and Russ Cameron for making me look good and my lovely wife for waiting patiently for me to write something that doesn't make her question the wisdom of saying 'yes' so many years ago. She's still waiting.

THE HANOVER BLOCK

i. long grass in autumn

Marion bought a blueberry donut from the vending machine and poured himself a Styrofoam cup full of thin coffee. The only other person in the break room was a guy with a bald spot, just another wrinkled white shirt talking on a cell phone, hiding his face in the corner.

Mr. Bald Spot didn't try to lower his voice, and either the volume on the phone was set to plus ten or he didn't know how to switch off speaker phone. Marion could hear every word the woman on the other end of the conversation was saying.

She wasn't happy. And there were kids involved.

Marion sat down, turned his back to the

guy, and tried not to listen.

But then Bald Spot's wife, or girlfriend, started accusing him of spending too much time in his new shed. She wanted to know if he was going out there to jerk off.

Marion knew then that he hadn't been noticed, because the guy didn't end the call. He didn't even turn around to see if anyone had overheard the accusation. He just whined into the phone, tried to defend himself, cooed at the woman with embarrassing pet names.

"I've been working on a project," Bald Spot said.

The woman screamed: "Bullshit! I haven't seen so much as a fucking model airplane!"

Marion had a bad feeling about where their conversation was headed. Even though he was in a break room open to all, he was worried that Mr. Bald Spot was going to realize he was there—very soon, and after something even more personal was discussed—and accuse him of eavesdropping on a private conversation.

Marion stood without moving his chair. He left the donut wrapper on the table instead of tossing it in the trash, afraid the crinkling plastic would give him away. He pulled open the break room door, slowly, knowing it had a tendency to creak.

He watched as he backed out into the hall, and Bald Spot never turned around. When Marion knew that he'd managed to exit without being noticed, the guy was still in the corner nuzzling his cell phone.

Only he wasn't talking anymore. He was crying.

Marion returned to his desk and shot off an e-mail to his boss in New York to let him know that he was leaving for the day. He'd written that he wasn't feeling well, which wasn't entirely a lie.

He couldn't quite figure out how he felt. But the word *malleable* kept coming to mind, which he knew couldn't be right. *Vulnerable,* too. Like the slightest thing could go wrong and he'd find himself in a psych ward.

He walked to his bus stop and wished he'd thought to check the schedule. He cleaned out his wallet while he waited, threw a condom and a health insurance card into a trashcan, both expired. There were no pictures in his wallet. He'd taken out the mini-folio with the plastic sleeves years ago. His old photos were in a lock-box now, and he wasn't even sure where he'd put the key.

He checked his wristwatch and a minute later wondered why he'd bothered; he wouldn't know if the buses were running late.

He cleared his pockets of old receipts, cigarette packaging foil and cellophane, found a comb he didn't know he had, ran it through his hair, and threw that in the trash, too.

The clouds were dark overhead, and it felt to Marion like it was much later in the day. It was like finding himself alone at twilight, when he should be surrounded by people. The world was stark, simplified in gray. Seedy smudges on the glass of the bus stop's weather shelter crystallized into complex patterns. Marion found himself searching for forms in the fingerprints, in the lipstick smears, in the streaks of nothing left by raindrops.

His mind had just conjured a nest of goblins hidden in what looked like a spray of chocolate milk when he heard the bus's brakes screech and sigh.

He didn't rush to climb aboard.

He swiped his pass and saw that the bus was empty of riders, that he could have whichever seat he wanted. But he chose the seat he got stuck with every day, near the back, right in front of the bus's rear doors, the place no one wanted because it was a high-traffic area.

When he took his seat, he noticed that the driver was missing. The bus was empty.

Then the driver stamped up the steps, as if he were knocking snow off his boots. He waved a fan of dollar bills at Marion and smiled.

"Five bucks," he called to the back of the bus, "just sitting by the trash can."

Marion had a feeling it was his money, that it had fallen to the ground when he was cleaning out his wallet, but he didn't say anything to the driver or bother to check. He didn't know how much cash he'd been carrying anyway.

The bus jerked forward.

Marion held tight to the metal grab handle above his seat—too tightly, he had to consciously loosen his grip—and the buildings become less and less modern and well-maintained as they rolled by.

The bus stopped a dozen times, but only one more rider climbed on, a young black man with white hair in a three-piece suit carrying a ceramic skull in a cardboard box. It was a cheap Halloween candle-holder. Its packaging was covered with cartoon spider webs and spooky lettering. He sat at the front of the bus and read from a hand-held device. He was still staring into it when Marion got off at his stop.

The doors hissed open and Marion stepped out onto the corner of Stokes and Fields, about eight blocks from his house. He sucked in the heat and smell wafting out from a rundown coin laundry's opened doors and lit up a smoke, just like he did every night. But it wasn't night now. It wasn't even noon. And though the lighting was the same as when he stepped off the bus at 5:45 in the evening, things were very different. There was less movement. The customers inside the laundry were old and tired, just going through the motions, more like ghosts trapped in glass than real people. The few stragglers he saw on the street kept to themselves or talked to themselves. When cars passed, it was like a calming whisper, so very different from the roar of rush hour.

Marion smoked and walked and thought

about the pillar of grass he knew he'd see upon turning the corner of Fields and Marshall. He'd been watching it grow since the beginning of summer, a four-foot high, not quite circular, tower of unmowed grass in almost the exact center of the front yard belonging to the house sitting at 279 Marshall Boulevard. He wondered if the pillar signified anything in the reputedly diseased mind of the house's occupant. A man named Calvin Carmichael was said to live alone in the house with only a single fat cat to keep him company. He was often overheard talking to the cat about baseball stats and intelligence agencies that he believed were competing against one another to see who could kill him the fastest.

There was an old dog standing on the corner of Fields and Marshall when Marion arrived, a spindly black Catahoula Leopard Dog with fur gone white around his whiskers. The dog stared down the street, transfixed by the pillar of grass. Or perhaps by the sight of old Calvin Carmichael mowing his lawn.

Marion stopped and stood a few yards back from the old dog and finished his smoke. He'd never seen Carmichael before. The man was shirtless, and the suspenders that held his pants up to his ribcage bisected his two over-sized man breasts into four. His beard was like filthy stuffed animal fillings and hung almost to the bottom of his sternum. He was bald on top, and the hair that grew from the base of his skull to the middle of his back was gray and loosely braided.

The man mowed in his bare feet. They were stained green and black. He pushed the mower back and forth toward the pillar, mowing in circles around it.

Marion threw down his cigarette butt and walked past the Catahoula. When he found himself standing on the sidewalk in front of Carmichael's house, he heard the dog's untrimmed nails skittering on the concrete behind him.

Carmichael turned and scowled. "Don't like dogs," he said. His voice was high-pitched, almost feminine. Marion hadn't been expecting that. "Get it out of here."

"It's not my dog," Marion shouted over the noise of the mower.

"Keep on walking," Carmichael said. "It followed you here, maybe it will follow you home."

"Can I ask you a question?" Marion asked.

"What?" Carmichael yelled. "Can't hear you over the mower." He continued mowing, back and forth, not even coming close to the pillar. Then he turned back, saw Marion and the strange dog still standing there, and switched off the mower.

"What the—?" he said, clenching his fists at waist level. "What?"

"I wanted to ask you about your lawn," Marion said.

Carmichael sidled up to the pillar of grass, waved his hands in the air, rotating the palms like an old-time movie director lining up a shot, then marched over to the sidewalk and put his hands on his hips. He thrust out his chin and smiled.

Calvin Carmichael had beautiful white teeth. They looked to Marion as if they were all capped.

Marion took a step back. The dog did, too.

"Can't you see I'm busy?" Carmichael said. "Don't have time to waste. Got things to do."

"I promise I'll only be a minute," Marion said. "I'm just curious."

"Your type always is," Carmichael said. "Which agency you with, anyway?"

"I live on Oakbend, just a few blocks from here."

"Don't mean you can't be CIA."

"Well, I'm not. I walk this way every day after getting off the bus."

"Bus, my ass. You're too old to be in school."

"I was talking about the metro."

"Oh," Carmichael said. "I might have known."

"Right," Marion said. "The long grass in the middle of your yard. I just thought it was interesting, that's all. Is it a sort of sculpture?"

Carmichael twisted his wrists and gave two thumbs down to the dog, turned around, and scanned the yard. "Don't know what you're talking about," he said. "There's no sculpture."

"No," Marion said. "I was talking about the four-foot high pillar of grass you have there. Why do you cut it that way?"

Carmichael shook his head. "Don't know what you're getting at, pal. Mow my lawn once a week."

Marion realized the old man didn't see the pillar. He had no idea it was there.

"OK," Marion said. "Sorry to bother you."

Carmichael stomped over to his mower and repeatedly yanked the pull-starter, cursing under his breath.

When the engine finally roared to life, he shouted over his shoulder, "And take that fucking dog with you!"

Marion walked on.

The dog stayed behind and stared at the grass, a thin line of drool drizzling to the concrete from his smiling chops.

The streets grew quieter the farther away he walked from Carmichael's house. A pack of truant kids rode by on bicycles, but they didn't call back and forth to one another as they pedaled. Dried leaves skittered across the streets. A band-saw whined from a distant garage.

When he turned off Marshall on to Fennington, the sun came out from behind the clouds, and he heard a lone hammer, pounding, steadily. He noticed a new shed in the backyard of one of the houses and stopped walking. Its position in the yard was peculiar. Instead of being built along the yard's back fence, where it would have fit naturally, it stood about fifteen feet from the house's back door, set at an odd angle.

Maybe it isn't anchored yet. It looks pretty lightweight. They could be moving it later.

Marion lit up another smoke and kept walking. He couldn't help but think of Mr. Bald Spot's cell phone conversation back at the office.

It could be someone's jerk-off palace.

The hammering grew louder as he approached Tredmore. When he turned the corner, he saw a teenager hammering a nail into a small wooden playhouse. Construction on it was almost complete. Only the roof needed to be nailed into place. The boy's father sat on the back porch with his arms crossed, a can of beer nestled in a cozy on a nearby wrought iron table.

The kid wielded his hammer with a vengeance, missing the nails half the time.

The playhouse stood along the back fence of their yard, but it wasn't facing toward the house. Instead, it stood just far enough back from the fence to allow the door to swing open.

The kid was too old for a playhouse. He had some fur on his chin and a small tattoo of a howling demoness on his right shoulder.

Marion didn't see any evidence of younger siblings in the yard: no abandoned toys or overturned tricycles. He couldn't remember ever seeing children playing here before.

Marion tried not to stare as he passed the house, but the kid's father was glaring at him. He picked up his pace until he was out of sight.

By the time he turned on to Oakbend, his

forehead was dripping. His shirt and pants were sticking to his skin when he stepped up to his mailbox. He sorted through the mail and dumped the junk into a trashcan still sitting at the end of his driveway from the trash pick-up two nights before—the lid strewn off into the middle of his yard—and carried the bills and the colorful payment past due notices inside.

The house was stuffy and he made a tour of the place to open the windows. There were too many rooms for him alone: four bedrooms, two baths, a den and an over-sized great room, but he couldn't bring himself to put it on the market. He told himself that it was sacrosanct, but he knew the truth was that he was just lazy.

He changed out of his work clothes into a pair of shorts and a black t-shirt and thought about making some lunch but grabbed a beer from the fridge instead and stepped out onto the back deck.

He sat on a metal rocking bench, put his feet up on a matching chair, and looked over into his neighbor's yard at the monstrosity under construction there. The man who lived next door had been working his kids nights and weekends for a month building a geodesic climbing dome. Now construction had begun on a second, larger climbing dome built up around the first. It looked like there would be an area of about three feet between them for the kids to wiggle around in.

Marion had been meaning to ask why they'd decided to go with the nested domes, but he didn't know them that well, and the guy who owned the place—he was pretty sure his name was Chuck—was kind of an asshole. He was always drunk and yelling at the kids. Rumor had it that the guy was a widower, left to raise three kids on his own; all boys between the ages of seven and thirteen, Marion guessed. He'd once seen Chuck line them up in the backyard with their pants down around their ankles and whack their bare asses with a PVC pipe. Their punishment had something to do with wasting shaving cream.

Marion turned his attention to Dale Grater's yard, his other next door neighbor, opposite Chuck. Dale had been erecting elaborate birdhouses on his property for years. They stood atop towering poles of varying heights throughout his backyard and all along his fence line. There were birdhouses modeled after all the major landmarks in the nation's capital: the White House, the Lincoln Memorial, and the Washington Monument. There were tee pees, pagodas, and pyramids, a miniature Eiffel Tower, the Taj Mahal, the Empire State Building, and most of the ruins from ancient Rome. There were birdhouse busts of famous people: the Marx Brothers, Elvis, Marilyn Monroe, W.C. Fields, Martin Luther King, Jr., and Benjamin Franklin. And there were busts of all the famous monsters of film-land, too: the Wolfman, Dracula. Frankenstein's Monster, the Creature from the Black Lagoon, the Mummy, the Phantom of the Opera. There was even a triffid birdhouse.

Several people in the neighborhood had complained to the city about Dale's backyard. They called it an eyesore. But nothing was done about it; he wasn't breaking any laws. And Marion's neighborhood didn't have a homeowner's association to field their grievances like most of the newer developments sprouting up from abandoned farmland on the other side of the highway.

Marion didn't mind the birdhouses themselves. It was the bird shit that got to him. The six-foot tall privacy fence that separated his property from Dale's was plastered with runnels of white.

Marion finished his beer and admired the way the noonday sun left his backyard empty of bizarre shadows. It wouldn't be long before they started creeping over the fence, invading his space. He had just a couple of hours left, then the pillars and birdhouse forms would twist across his lawn into a dark field of silhouettes—heads on pikes and wicked scarecrows, impaled mythological beasts and human corpses.

ii. the neighborhood peeper returns

Marion called in sick the next day. He couldn't imagine going through the trouble of showering, getting dressed, and walking to the bus stop. He'd woken sweaty and confused. And so very tired. He'd shuffled to his home office, lightheaded, and struggled through every step in the simple process of typing and sending an e-mail to his boss.

He pulled on yesterday's wrinkled clothes and walked two blocks over to Buddy Harper's house to buy some pot. He'd grown up with Buddy and started buying from him in high school. Ever since he was busted for dealing in his early twenties, Buddy only allowed foot traffic from his customers. And you weren't permitted to call him on the phone to see if he was home before stopping by.

But Buddy was always home. He had an extensive growing lab hidden behind a wall in his basement, and he spent most of his time down there tending to his plants.

A cool breeze made Marion wish he'd worn a light jacket. A mail truck stuttered by, up-shifting and downshifting with groans and gasps, as it traveled between mailboxes. A lone dachshund barked at him from behind a chain-linked fence. A city worker filled a pothole with gravel while two of his co-workers looked on, smoking cigarettes, their truck idling in the middle of the street.

Buddy's house needed a coat of paint, and the vinyl siding was crooked in spots. The grass was overgrown. Only weeds grew in the flowerbeds. The front door was scarred with scratches from a dog who'd been dead for years.

Marion rang the doorbell and waited.

And waited.

He rang the bell again, lit up a smoke, and sat on the front step.

Buddy's neighbor across the street came out to check the mail. She was a heavyset woman in her mid-forties. Her perm was frazzled, the artificial color faded to reveal patches of shiny gray, and her jowls quivered when she walked. She obviously didn't approve of Marion sitting there. She carried her stack of unruly catalogs and glossy circulars back into the house and looked back over her shoulder at Marion three times before slamming her door shut.

Marion was about to try the doorbell one last time when Buddy pulled up in a dented and rusted four-door sedan.

Marion wondered why he hadn't noticed that Buddy's car wasn't parked in the driveway. He blamed it on not being fully awake.

Buddy climbed out of the car and looked up and down the street before smiling over at Marion, displaying a butter tooth he'd had since grade school. "Playing hooky?" he asked Marion.

"No," Marion lied. "I had a three-day weekend coming to me."

"That's good," Buddy said. "You've been needing the time off."

"I just wish it were longer."

"I hear you." Buddy closed the driver's side door and opened the trunk. "Well, you arrived just in time. I got me a little picnic all set up in the backyard."

"A picnic? It's not even noon."

"You can't have a breakfast picnic?"

"I suppose you can. But it is a bit strange."

"What's strange about it?"

"A man having a breakfast picnic alone in his backyard."

"Who says I'll be eating alone?" Buddy closed the trunk. He clutched a brown paper bag to his chest.

"If you have company, I can go," Marion

said. If Buddy were entertaining a female house guest, he didn't want to intrude. Buddy didn't have many girlfriends and Marion didn't want to mess things up.

"No, stay. There's no one here. I just got a wild hair up my ass, is all."

Buddy walked up to the porch, shifted the bag from his right arm to his left, and extended his hand.

Marion stood and shook.

"How've you been?" Buddy asked. "You don't look so good."

"Thanks. I appreciate it."

"Seriously. You been sick?"

"No. I'm fine. Just tired. Been working a ton of extra hours."

"It sounds to me like a nice little breakfast picnic is exactly what you need. Come on around back."

Buddy led them to a splintery wooden gate and handed the bag over to Marion while he unfastened the lock.

"I was just about ready to eat when I realized that I needed something special to drink." Buddy waved Marion through the gate and reclaimed the bag. "You ever have mimosa?" he asked.

"Isn't that champagne and OJ?"

"Yeah."

"No."

"I haven't had it before either. Always

curious about it though. Thought this was the perfect occasion to try it."

"What's the occasion? It's not your birthday." Marion was pretty certain that Buddy had been born in the spring.

"No," Buddy said. "It's my very first picnic."

"You spend too much time alone."

Buddy laughed.

An old bed sheet was spread out in the grass a few feet from Buddy's cracked concrete patio. It must have been thirty years old with its faded pattern of rocket ships, bug-eyed aliens, and buxom damsels in distress wearing what looked like nightgowns with giant stiff collars. Resting at its center was a tarnished silver platter with a domed lid. There were Tupperware containers weighing down all four corners and two place settings. Each plate and piece of silverware appeared to be from different sets.

Marion pointed at the place settings and said, "I thought you said you didn't have company."

"I don't. I set it for two out of a need for symmetry."

"Oh, I thought you just wanted to seem more lonely and pathetic."

"That, too." Buddy sat down on the sheet and unloaded a bottle of champagne and a gallon jug of orange juice from his brown paper bag. "Since you're still standing," he said, peeling the top of a Tupperware container to reveal a jumble of fried onions, peppers, and scrambled eggs, "would you mind running in and getting a couple of flutes? They're in the hutch in the foyer."

"Champagne flutes?"

"No, musical instruments. I was planning on seducing you with a serenade."

"Fancy."

"The door's locked." Buddy extended his legs, reached into a front pants pocket, and threw Marion his key chain. "And don't steal anything while you're in there."

Marion knew Buddy was only half joking with his stealing comment. Paranoia was natural in his line of work.

Marion stepped through the back door into the kitchen and was overtaken by the smell of layer upon layer of cloistered human habitation. It was hard to breathe the air, dusty and thick with dirty laundry, rotting food, spilled beer and stale smoke. The breakfast table was stacked high with grimy plates, bills, and junk mail. The sink was filled with pots and pans. An old refrigerator stopped humming as he walked past, leaving behind an eerie silence.

The hallway that led to the foyer was littered with mismatched shoes and rolled-up socks. An old tandem bike with two flat tires leaned against a wall.

Marion opened the hutch's glass doors. There didn't seem to be a complete set of anything inside. It appeared that as wine glasses and water goblets shattered throughout the years, nothing had been replaced. He found the champagne flutes tucked behind a Mad Hatter cookie jar and returned with them to the kitchen.

He stopped before opening the back door and watched Buddy through the kitchen window above the sink. He was out there snatching at flies or gnats.

Probably gnats.

Whatever they were, Marion couldn't see them from where he stood. It looked like, after grabbing the insects from the air, Buddy was shoving them into his mouth.

Marion leaned forward over the sink.

Buddy grabbed another insect and struggled to pull it from the air, as if the gnat were tethered by an invisible wire and had to be ripped free. And, again, it appeared that he popped the insect into his mouth like a piece of popcorn.

No.

The action was more like a riveted movie-goer inhaling a fistful of popcorn.

Marion looked away, embarrassed for his old friend.

He also didn't want to be caught staring through the window. He shifted the glasses to his left hand and pulled open the door. The fresh autumn air cleansed him as he stepped outside, peeled from his skin the residue left by Buddy's life inside his cave.

"Here we go," Marion said, holding up the

champagne flutes. "Let's start mixing that mimosa." He didn't want to mention the gnats; Buddy's mood would sour if he thought he'd been spied on.

Marion sat in the grass and placed the flutes on the silver tray to provide some stability for the pouring.

"You have any idea what ratio you're supposed to use?" Marion asked. He scooped out some eggs onto his plate, speared a sausage link and took a bite. It was warm and tasted fine. Although he was concerned about food poisoning, based on the state of Buddy's kitchen.

"Yeah." Buddy broke the seal on the orange juice container. "We're talking three parts champagne, one part OJ." He poured a dabble of juice into the glasses. "I found the recipe on the back of some old lounge music compilation."

Marion watched Buddy uncoil the wire on the champagne bottle and noticed that Buddy's fingernails were overgrown and filthy.

"That's what we need," Buddy said.

"What?"

"A little music." Buddy popped the cork and it went flying into the yard. "Would you mind grabbing that for me? I'm going to run inside real quick."

Marion crawled into the yard and retrieved the cork while Buddy disappeared into the house.

A minute later, Buddy returned with another Tupperware container and a miniature CD player. He took his place on the bed sheet and switched it on. Surf guitar filled the air.

"That's better." Buddy poured the champagne and handed a glass to Marion. "Let's have a toast."

"To what?"

"To being confident in our heterosexuality."

"Yeah. I hope no one's hiding in the bushes taking pictures."

They clinked their glasses together and sampled the mimosa.

"That reminds me," Buddy said. "Trevor Cadwallader's in town for a while."

"They let him out of jail?"

"He hasn't been in jail for a long time now."

"I haven't seen the guy in over a decade," Marion said. And the truth was he hadn't missed him. Cadwallader gave him the creeps, even before he'd been arrested and exposed as the neighborhood's peeping Tom. Rumor had it that Trevor had been tracking cheating spouses and snapping pictures with some grandiose blackmailing scheme in mind. "I just kind of assumed he was in jail for something."

"No. He's gainfully employed, surprisingly enough. He travels all over now. He's some kind of IT contractor, laying cable for new office buildings. I think that's what he said. I really don't know what that means. Shit, I don't know anything about that kind of shit."

"I'm glad to hear he's given up sneaking

around in backyards." Marion buttered a biscuit.

"I wouldn't say that," Buddy said. "From what he tells me, he's just gotten better at it. I guess he's got pictures of all kinds of crazy shit, from backyards all over the country. Video, too."

"The guy's sick."

"He's not that bad. Just eccentric. He calls his little adventures 'anthropological research.'"

"I'm sure he does."

"He does have a lot of nudie pictures in his collection, from what I understand. But he says he also has pictures of some shit you wouldn't believe."

"Yeah?"

"Oh, yeah. When he was out in LA, he got some snapshots of this cosmetic surgeon's dog. I guess the guy's been operating on his pooch for years. He says the poor thing's face is almost human."

"Come on."

"He's got pictures."

"And photo editing software."

"Maybe. He says he's got video of some Mormons out in Utah performing some kind of black mass."

"Bullshit."

"We're not talking the head of the church here."

"I'm still not buying it."

"He says he's got all kinds of gadgets now. Night vision goggles. Mini spy cams. Hovering saucers to get over fences. He's even got one of those huge remote controlled planes, like the ones you see those fat guys flying down at Rydall Park, outfitted with a telescopic lens."

"Is it a stealth bomber?"

"You know, I asked him that. He said they can't get remote-controlled planes to fly with that body type. He's looked into it. It's a Corsair.

"He says he's invented a spy camera that he can destroy from a distance with just the press of a button."

"He must be making pretty good money," Marion said. "You're talking about some pretty expensive hardware."

"I think he is. Besides, he doesn't have a wife and kids to worry about. And he lives alone."

"Yeah." Marion moved the eggs around on his plate with his fork and mixed himself another mimosa, concentrating intently on getting the champagne-to-orange-juice ratio just right.

Buddy returned to his breakfast and chewed with his mouth open, a ridiculous mockery of a thoughtful expression on his face. He examined the clouds, the trees, the grass, as if he were one to be deeply affected by the simple pleasures of nature.

They sat in uncomfortable silence until they were finished eating.

Marion wiped his lips with a paper napkin and said, "He didn't show you any of this stuff when you saw him. I'm assuming he didn't tell you all this over the phone."

"Oh, no," Buddy said. "You know how I am about the phone. And, no. I didn't actually see any of the stuff. I ran into him outside the laundry mat."

"He told you all that outside the laundry mat?"

"No, we ended up going to The Old Redface across the street for a drink. But I am supposed to go over to his place this weekend. You're welcome to come along."

"I don't know."

"He's staying in a condo just over on Aberdeen."

"Maybe. Call me when you're going over. I might join you." Marion had no intention of paying Trevor Cadwallader any visits.

"You won't go."

"I might."

"I'll call you anyway." Buddy peeled open the small Tupperware container he'd brought out with the miniature CD player. "You want to smoke a joint?"

"Why not?" The bottom of the Tupperware container was filled with what appeared to be cigarettes. Buddy spent hours with his rolling machine assembling his 'outside' joints, a blend of finely ground pot and cheap, but fragrant, tobacco. They looked perfect, too.

Buddy handed one over, and Marion lit up. He coughed. The harshness of the tobacco always caught him by surprise.

"Careful there," Buddy said. "It's pretty strong stuff. You don't have to hold it in. Just smoke it like you would a regular smoke."

"Yeah, yeah," Marion said, taking another drag.

Buddy lit up his own filtered joint and surveyed the remains of his breakfast picnic. "What a mess," he said. "I don't think I'll be doing this again any time soon."

"I'll help you clean up."

"That's all right. I've got to clean my kitchen before I can even start on this. I wouldn't put you through that."

"I was just in there. Thanks for having mercy on me."

"Fuck you. Are you going to buy a bag or what?"

"Yeah. How much?"

"The usual."

Marion reached into the right front pocket of his jeans, palmed the wad of bills he'd tucked there, grabbed a cloth napkin, pretended to wipe his lips with it, then placed the napkin at the center of the bed sheet with the money hidden underneath.

Buddy smiled, nodded, and repeated the same routine with the bag of pot he'd stuffed into his shirt pocket.

They finished their joints, had a couple more rounds of mimosa, argued about movies they'd recently seen, discretely traded napkins, and said their goodbyes.

Buddy's neighbor from across the street was outside again, sweeping leaves and dirt from her driveway. The broom's brush was over-sized and wild with twisted and broken bristles. Her garage door was open. Its interior had been converted into a lushly furnished Victorian sitting room. When she spotted Marion, she stopped sweeping, produced a key-chain, and depressed a button that closed the garage door. She swiveled--only her upper body following him--the broom propped on her shoulder like a rifle.

When he turned the corner, she was still watching him.

An abandoned mail truck was idling in the middle of the street, wildly parked, blocking both lanes. Marion surveyed the street and there was no sign of a mail carrier.

The city guys were still patching the same pothole. And it was the same guy as before doing all the work. He smeared tar over the gravel in a soaking t-shirt, the top of his uniform tied around his head to catch the sweat, while his co-workers tossed a cracked and filthy whiffle ball back and forth.

Marion walked on in the direction of the barking dachshund, but when he arrived at the fenced yard where the dog had been, it was empty. A dog collar lay on the ground at the end of a staked chain. He could still hear the dog barking somewhere close by, very close, like it had slipped into a pocket universe from which only sound escapes.

Marion stopped to light a smoke and noticed the cloud cover overhead cast a distinct separation of light and a false twilight on the street thirty yards from where he stood. He walked toward the shadow wall, but it was ever shifting, and he knew, even if he ran, he'd never cross the threshold.

A white sedan with tinted windows emerged from the semi-darkness and slowed down, almost to a stop, as it passed Marion. Suspicious of the driver's intentions, he felt his adrenaline surge.

He was thankful for the alcohol in his system, for the artificial bravery it provided. It tempered the paranoia brought on by the pot.

If he hadn't drank the mimosa, he knew he'd be in a state of near panic when he arrived at his home a few minutes later to find a police car parked in front of his house.

Marion climbed his front steps and fumbled with his keys. He could smell the cruiser's exhaust, hear voices on the police radio talking between bursts of static. When he finally got the door opened, the police car was still sitting there.

After he'd visited the bathroom and the fridge to grab a beer, he peeked through the blinds. Another police cruiser had joined the first. But he didn't see any officers outside the vehicles.

Marion drank his beer. Ten minutes later, after he'd poured the last bitter dregs down his throat, the cops pulled away. Slowly, they drove up the street, side by side, blocking both lanes of traffic.

He grabbed another beer and sat on his back deck to have a smoke. A plaid autumn jacket was draped over a bar at the top of Chuck's climbing domes. The jungle gyms cast a web of shadows over the grass, and the jacket became a giant spider waiting at its center.

Marion smoked half the cigarette and went back inside.

He didn't like spiders.

iii. advanced voyeurism

Trevor's condo was within walking distance, but Buddy drove over anyway. He didn't want to leave his car in his driveway and have people stopping by and hanging out on his front step, thinking he was home.

He parked, retrieved a bottle of rum from the back seat, and walked up the steps to Trevor's building. Eight units were split between two stories, and Trevor was renting one on the first floor, on the back right side of the building. He never rented a place above ground level, in case of fires.

Buddy stepped into a small glass-enclosed lobby and pressed a button labeled 2G.

"Buddy?" came a voice through the wall-mounted speaker.

"Trevor?" Buddy said.

The door buzzed, and the lock disengaged. He rushed to open the door before the lock clicked shut again, knowing these setups left you with the narrowest window of opportunity.

Buddy thought back to a night when he'd been drunk, trapped in the lobby of an apartment building, trying to beat the buzzer on one of these damned doors while his girlfriend waited upstairs. That night had been the beginning of the end of that relationship. And in the back of his mind, he always thought that it was partly because she'd lost the mood during the little comedy show in her building's lobby.

Buzz.

"Shit," Buddy remembered himself saying a dozen times, running back and forth to the intercom, depressing the button. "I missed it again, sweetheart."

Back and forth, back and forth.

Buzz.

"Shit."

Buzz.

"Shit."

Buzzzzzz...

Tonight, Buddy was relieved to have made it through on the first buzz. He found 2G and knocked. He heard what sounded like an electric drill winding down then approaching footsteps.

Trevor opened the door, and he stood there grinning, thin lips disappearing around a set of perfect little teeth. His black hair was long and stringy, tucked behind pointed ears. His elfin face had the smoothness of someone who doesn't have to shave. His arched eyebrows were the kind coveted by cover girls. His hunched posture made him look as if he were sneaking everywhere. It didn't help that he always dressed in black. On this night, he wore a black sweatshirt and a brand new pair of black jeans. The white rubber on his black canvas sneakers had been colored in with a permanent marker. His eyes were black, too, and they sparkled with glints of dangerous intellect and secret mischief.

"Come on in, man," Trevor said. He opened the door wide, turned his back to Buddy, and returned to a workbench he'd built out of particleboard and a couple of saw horses. He picked up an electric screwdriver and finished installing a motherboard into a bulky laptop.

Buddy closed the door, locked the handle, turned the deadbolt, and slid the chain into its slot.

"What the hell kind of laptop is that?" Buddy asked. "The thing looks like it weighs thirty pounds."

"It's actually pretty lightweight, considering. It's military issue. It was designed to survive a drop from a two-story building. It's fireproof and bulletproof, too."

"Where'd you get it?"

"From an army surplus store in Tucson."

"I'm surprised they'd sell something like that."

"I was, too. They didn't even wipe the hard drive properly. There was all kinds of shit still on it that shouldn't have been."

"Like what?"

"Nothing earthshattering. Nothing like evidence of space aliens or anything like that. Just mission details from some black ops. Troop coordinates. But I wiped it all, and I did it right. The last thing I need is to be caught with that shit."

"Yeah." Buddy unloaded his bottle of rum onto the workbench and twisted open the cap.

"You mind putting that on the kitchen table?" Trevor said. "I got a lot of expensive shit in here."

"Sure. Sorry."

"Don't be sorry. Just get it off the bench."

Buddy picked up the bottle and headed for the kitchen. There were boxes everywhere, some opened and overflowing with clothes and magazines and books, some still sealed shut. There was no conventional furniture in the place: a few lawn chairs, an undressed mattress with a sleeping bag unrolled over it, a cushion from a couch that was nowhere to be seen. There were two more makeshift workbenches in the room, covered with small electronic parts that Buddy had no hope of identifying. A teetering bookshelf made from plywood and cinder blocks housed a wealth of reference material on spy-craft, hacking, and information security. Trevor's remote control Corsair rested atop a card table. A forty-two inch wide-screen plasma TV hung on one wall above an oversized beanbag chair, next to which sat a table made for toddlers. There were a few empty beer bottles on the little table and a plastic bowl filled with peanut shells. A dozen glossy S&M porn mags were strewn across the carpet, along with pizza boxes, root beer cans, and what appeared to be the husks of hundreds of gutted toys. Buddy guessed it was their innards that were strewn across Trevor's workbenches.

Buddy stepped over an opened toolbox and a half-dozen disassembled desktop PCs on his way to the kitchen, careful not to step on the countless compact disks scattered everywhere. He switched on the kitchen light and found a wooden bench tucked in next to a frayed wicker table. The tabletop was clear save for a single bag of unopened potato crisps. More electronics and dirty dishes covered the counter tops. The top of a small fridge—something Buddy would expect to find in a college dorm room—was stacked high with cereal boxes and snacks.

He set the bottle of rum on the table and went in search of drinking glasses. He opened every cabinet and found two more laptops, an array of teeny video cameras, a fireproof safe, coils of Ethernet cables, and two sets of night-vision goggles, before he found anything he'd expected to find in a kitchen. Only one door revealed a collection of mismatched plates and bowls and a dozen plastic cups covered with cartoon characters and sports team logos, the kind of cups you'd get with up-sized meals at fast food restaurants.

Near the back of the cabinet, he found a single shot glass. It had the Jolly Roger stamped on it and looked clean. He set that on the table for later, filled two cups with ice, mixed the rum with some root beer, and returned to the living room.

Trevor sat in the beanbag chair with a laptop in his lap and a wireless trackball mouse on a TV tray to his right. The plasma TV on the wall was turned on now and Trevor had the laptop hooked up to it. He scrolled through thousands of files. Their names spun by so fast that Buddy couldn't read any of them.

"Have a seat," Trevor said. "I've got some good shit to show you."

Buddy sat in a deck chair next to the kiddie table and offered a cup to Trevor.

"Just set it on down there," Trevor said, cocking his head to one side, searching, searching. "Here we go."

He double-clicked and the TV screen filled with an overhead shot of a woman sunbathing nude next to a kidney-shaped swimming pool.

"Nice," Buddy said, sipping his drink. The woman was a good looking blonde with huge tits. "Very nice. How'd you get that?"

Trevor jerked a thumb over his shoulder and said, "I've got a little hover drone. I usually scout out an area with the Corsair, then send the hover drone out for extended shots, if I find something good." He picked up his drink and swirled the ice around. "Keep watching."

Buddy kept watching. For a minute, that seemed like five, nothing much happened. He was just watching a naked woman lying out in the sun. Then he saw it. Something big moved into the scene.

"What the hell is that?" Buddy asked, leaning forward.

"What's it look like?"

"Some dude in a giant dinosaur costume. Like one of those mascots at an amusement park."

"It's a dragon, actually. Blaze the Dragon. From Thunder Island, up in Michigan."

The dragon approached the blonde. She stood and wrapped her arms around the thing's non-existent neck, then turned away, bent over and pressed her ass into the dragon's belly.

From the bird's-eye view, Buddy couldn't tell if the guy in the dragon costume had opened a flap at his crotch and was actually doing what it looked like he was doing.

"Is he actually getting her from behind?"

"Yeah. You can't really tell in this video, but he is."

The dragon continued to thrust for a few more minutes, and when he was finished, he pushed the blonde into the pool.

"That was rude," Buddy said, laughing.

"Oh, she doesn't mind." Trevor was rolling a joint now. "It's all part of their little ritual. I've got stills from other sessions I could show you. This was the only time I was able to record the whole thing. Technical problems."

"Who the hell are these people?"

"Actually, he's the official Blaze the Dragon. Been doing it for fifteen years or so. She's just a groupie."

"You're shitting me."

"No. There really are Blaze groupies out there."

"I can't imagine there are very many."

"You'd be surprised." Trevor closed out of the Blaze the Dragon Sex Show and double-clicked on another file.

The screen displayed video shot through a night-vision lens that turned everything green and otherworldly. A group of people stood in a circle. The men wore shirts and ties and the women were covered in conservative dresses. They all faced an effigy of Christ nailed upside-down to a rickety wooden structure, two interlocking squares that formed an eight-pointed star.

"This is that Mormon black mass I was telling you about." Trevor lit one end of the joint and took a deep drag before handing it to Buddy. "Sorry. There's no audio."

Buddy took a hit, holding in the smoke

when he said, "Are you sure these guys are real Mormons?"

"Well, they claim to be."

Buddy exhaled. The joint petered out, and he lit it up again.

A man on the screen stepped forward with a torch, touched it to the wooden structure, and it burst into flames.

Buddy took another drag.

"But obviously they're not real Mormons," Trevor said. He took the joint from Buddy and tapped the ashes off into an empty root beer can. "Real Mormons don't hold black masses."

The man with the torch turned away from the burning Christ. His face twisted into a scream, and he pointed directly at the camera. The circle broke, and people started running. Including the cameraman. The screen filled with trees whizzing past, branches slapping against the camera's lens, then shoes running over leaves and grass. Then blackness.

"Wow," Buddy said. "They fucking caught your ass."

"No. But they tried. They even shot at me a couple times."

"No shit?"

"Yeah. It was a pretty fucked up situation."

"How'd they know you were there?"

"I fucking sneezed." Trevor sniffled. "Fucking allergies."

iv. shithole

People weren't sending e-mails with subject lines anymore. Or the subject lines didn't make sense. The contents of most replies didn't answer (or were absolutely unrelated to) the questions he'd asked. Almost every message Marion received was nearly unreadable, sent by persons who claimed not to comprehend the perfectly reasonable e-mails he'd sent them.

He hated typos. Incomplete sentences. Sentences that weren't capitalized. Fancy fonts and cutesy backgrounds. He hated blinking signatures and their inspirational footers.

Failures can't say they never tried!

He hated e-mail. But he hated instant

messaging more. He knew no one believed his complaints about the company's approved messaging application never working right on his laptop, and he didn't care. His lies got him out of using the damned thing.

Marion spent the second half of his morning writing vicious replies to all of his stupid e-mails. But he didn't send any of them. The thrill of accidentally hitting the Send button made his palms sweat. It was the most fun he'd had at work in a long time.

At noon, he walked across the street to a gourmet hot dog place and sat at the counter surrounded by shaggy-headed kids dressed in black. He ate a plain hot dog and stale potato chips. He washed it down with a bottle of orange soda then went outside to have a cigarette.

He watched people through the curling smoke. The sky was overcast and the sidewalk traffic was unhappy and gray. Every pore in every face was magnified, like the horrifying images of skin diseases found in a dermatologist's desk reference. He saw only disfiguring birthmarks and odd physiques. One in five people seemed to have a limp or a club foot.

An ape-like man in a muscle shirt stomped by, shaking a dented can of pink spray paint over his head. An emaciated girl, pimply, no older than fourteen, fluttered in the breeze, wearing a toucan-print muumuu. A struggling hunchback—a woman hugging a broken, shadeless desk lamp to her chest—coughed into a bloody handkerchief and nearly tripped over her own feet. A parade of elderly men shuffled past, a company of creeping question marks. Then came a gang of pear-shaped young boys, dressed in faded denim jackets riddled with vulgar iron-on patches. Every kid's haircut looked like a do-it-yourself job executed with rusty clippers.

When a seemingly normal suburban family walked by and broke up the parade of the downtrodden—mom and dad and their little boy—Marion dropped his unfinished cigarette into a sewer grate and fixated on the sparks and ashes tumbling into darkness.

Back in his office building, Marion rode the elevator up to the fifth floor, watched the only other rider disembark, then realized he'd forgotten to press any buttons, and had to ride down to ground level again.

When he finally reached the sixth floor, he went to the restroom for a piss, took his time washing and drying his hands, then stopped by the break room and leisurely mixed the sugar and non-dairy creamer into a cup of coffee poured from a carafe that had been sitting on the burner since 7 AM. He went by the mail pigeon holes, something he rarely did, and checked to make sure his slot was still empty. It was.

He toured the north side of the building—

his cubicle was on the south side—and found his friend Walter's desk empty, dashing his hopes of killing a few more minutes with idle chatter.

With no other stalling tactics coming to mind, Marion returned to his desk. Smiling to himself, he re-read and deleted the drafts of the e-mail replies he'd written that morning and, after slowly drinking half a cup of bitter coffee, he began the drudgery of composing civil and diplomatic responses to every single idiotic message in his Inbox.

He spent the remainder of his afternoon waiting for reports to run, scrubbing data, and sending the completed reports off to people across the globe whose faces he'd never seen.

The bus ride home seemed slower than usual, though there were no visible traffic issues and it was the regular driver. Part of it was due to the fact that a man who smelled of rotten cheese took the seat next to him. The man didn't look like he would emit an awful odor, but he did. He was dressed in a suit and tie, a neatly pressed shirt, and wore his hair slicked back with some stiffening goop, and he had a neatly trimmed beard. His forehead was thick with veins, and his face was twisted into a perpetual scowl. He looked like a stereotypical thug, mean by nature, but he talked mostly of role-playing games and comic books to someone through the headset tethered to his cell phone for almost the entire ride. His voice was nasally and soft, his tone pleasant. Marion guessed that the guy suffered from some bizarre neurosis which prevented him from ever touching his private parts with soap and water.

Thankfully, Cheesedick disembarked after a few stops, and Marion was able to catch his breath and settle his stomach before he climbed off the bus and was blasted with the overwhelming smells of the laundry mat.

He followed the usual route home, smoking along the way. When he turned the corner onto Marshall, he saw Carmichael's ever-rising pillar of grass. Right next to it stood a new structure.

Carmichael himself was nowhere to be seen. As Marion got closer, he saw that the tiny building was an old-fashioned outhouse. Merely decorative, he hoped. When he was a driveway or two down the block, he could see a sign nailed to the outhouse door. The sign read:

SHITHOLE

"Great, isn't it?" came a throaty female voice from behind Marion. He turned and saw a woman standing by a mailbox across the street, sucking on a stick of black licorice. She was maybe in her early thirties. It was hard to tell. Her face had the beginnings of the leather masks worn by life-long tanning bed enthusiasts. Her hair was dirty blonde, or just blonde and dirty, and she wore only a silk bathrobe loosely tied at her waist. It was obvious that she was wearing nothing underneath. Her naked flesh was exposed in places where he would have expected to see the straps and fasteners of undergarments. Her robe was cinched just above her left hipbone and served to just barely cover her pubis. Her breasts were plainly visible, except for the hardened nipples, which seemed to be the only things keeping the garment from slipping off onto the sidewalk.

"Yeah," Marion said. "Just great. When did he put that thing up? I was just by here on Thursday and it wasn't here then."

"Oh, let me think," she said, pushing the licorice deeper into her mouth. She hummed as she thought. Her lips pressed firmly against the candy as she pulled it from her mouth to say, "Saturday night. Well, early Sunday, really. He was out here hammering away at two o'clock in the morning."

"Did you call the cops?"

"Nah. I stay up late. Plus—" She snapped off a bit of licorice with her teeth. "I was occupied at the time."

"I'm surprised no one else called them," Marion said.

"The cops haven't done a thing about old Calvin, ever. Why should they start now?"

"Yeah. But that sign. That's got to be some kind of violation."

"You'd think so. But no one's cared enough to come out and make him take it down."

They stood in silence for a moment—

Marion sucking his smoke, the woman sucking her licorice—and marveled at the shithole on Calvin Carmichael's front lawn. Then she cleared her throat and said, "The poor old crazy fucker's got cancer, you know."

"No," Marion said. "No. I didn't."

"Some kind of rare shit I can't even pronounce. And he hates doctors. So he's not getting treatment." She flipped open the door on her mailbox, reached inside and pulled out a stack of magazines wrapped in plain brown paper. "I think people stopped complaining 'cause he's dying. Not out of sympathy or respect or anything. I think they've decided just to wait it out." The act of tucking her mail under her arm revealed her left breast and that she was shaved down below.

Marion didn't look away. What was exposed to him barely registered in his mind. His thoughts were occupied with disease and death. And by the time he realized that he probably should have looked away, it was already too late.

She winked and smiled at Marion as she covered herself again, and said, "Yeah, well, we'll all have a new neighbor soon enough."

v. crawling inside

Marion jerked upright. He wasn't breathing. He jumped out of bed and, either through some panicked, instinctual constriction of muscles, or the power of sheer will, he didn't know which, managed to force air into his lungs. His heart raced. He was sweaty and cold. Two words kept flashing in his mind.

Sleep apnea. Sleep apnea.

He sat on the bed, inhaled and exhaled, over and over again, to make sure everything was in working order, thinking that he was too young and not overweight enough to suffer from sleep apnea. But he really didn't know enough about the condition to make a self-diagnosis.

He thought he should probably see a doctor, a specialist, but knew that he wouldn't unless it happened again.

And again.

He ran his hands over his face and found something sticky under his nose, webbed across the left side of his face. His fingertips came away with blood.

His pillowcase was blotchy.

He'd had a nosebleed in the night. This had happened to him before. The dry air of late autumn brought them on. He'd suffered from them since early childhood. But they always woke him, and he'd run to the bathroom to plug up his nose and wait for the bleeding to stop. He'd never slept through one before.

He had to get cleaned up.

In the bathroom, he stood with his arms hanging at his sides, eyes and mouth closed, with his face turned up to meet the spray from the shower head. The temperature was near scalding, and the water pressure was fantastic. He stood like that for a long time and tried not to think, using pain as a distraction, willing the pulse of the water to seal his ears to the world.

He shivered as he dried himself off. He smeared on some deodorant and quickly dressed, brushed his teeth and hair. He didn't like what he saw in the mirror above the sink and didn't dwell on it.

He went outside for his morning smoke.

It was still dark at 6 AM. He sat in his usual spot on the wrought iron rocking bench, with his feet propped up on a matching chair, and lit up. The smoke curled and disappeared as it passed through a streetlight. A persistent flapping sound caught his attention.

He looked over at Dale's yard and noticed that he'd strung hundreds of plastic Halloween bats between the birdhouses. They snapped in the wind like the flags over a used car dealer's lot. Dale strung the bats year after year and didn't seem to care that the strings inevitably winged a few of the birds that his elaborate backyard haven sought to attract.

Marion turned his attention to Chuck's yard and saw a black mound where he expected the nested climbing domes to be. Its surface was shiny and reflected the streetlights and the light of the moon. It rustled in the wind, shivered and pulsed in the darkness, like an over-sized internal organ, a great diseased liver. He stood up and walked to the edge of the deck.

Chuck had covered the outer climbing dome with what looked like several camping tarps stitched together. It was hard to tell in the dark. But Marion could see that the edges of the tarps were tied down to stakes pounded in the ground around the perimeter. A bulge in the canvas moved like the head of a drunken mole in a Saturday morning cartoon, randomly disturbing earth as it struggles to find its way.

A flap opened at the base of the black mound and an arm poked free, then another. His neighbor Chuck crawled out onto the grass, struggling to catch his breath.

Marion considered retreating to the house, ducking down out of sight, but didn't.

Chuck lay on the grass, completely naked, eyes closed, chest heaving. His pale skin glistened with sweat.

A light switched on in a second story window of Chuck's house. As if sensing this, Chuck's eyes flipped open. He jumped to his feet, reached inside the tarp, retrieved a bathrobe, pulled it over his shoulders and cinched it at the waist. He tied the tarp back in place at the base of the dome and rushed inside. He didn't once look over in Marion's direction.

Loud crashing sounds came from Chuck's house, as if the man had stumbled into a pyramid of stacked pots and pans. This was followed by voices, loud curses, shouting.

Marion lit another smoke. The sun crested the top of the black dome, creating a nimbus of color as it turned the dew drops beaded across its surface into thousands of tiny prisms.

vi. levitation

Buddy sat next to Trevor in the dark. They had a giant can of kettle corn between them, and they were both munching away, staring up at the plasma screen, chomping and smacking their lips, eyes fixed to a rectangle of twilight sky framed with autumn branches.

Buddy thought back to when he was a kid, sprawled out in his foster mom's garden, leaves falling on his face, and huffing the smell of a distant bonfire with great satisfaction.

"I had the camera buried in this guy's backyard," Trevor said. "Got it there pretending to be one of his termite guys baiting traps."

"This isn't another fucking 'levitation'

video, is it?" Buddy asked.

"What's wrong with the 'levitation' videos?"

"Nobody's levitating. It just looks like a bunch of lonely fuckwads crawling up little invisible hillsides to me. Like some cheap-ass green screen effects."

"It's the last one," Trevor said. "And the shit's real."

"Bullshit."

"I shot the shit myself."

"Whatever you say." A naked man crawled across the plasma screen like a spider trapped behind the glass. *Another 'levitation' video*, Buddy thought, *just shot from a more extreme angle.* "This is getting pretty dull."

"Just wait a minute."

When the naked man reached the center of the screen (hovering about fifteen feet directly above the buried camera), his penis became erect, and he began thrusting wildly downward into Trevor's living room.

"Next," Buddy said.

"What do you mean?"

"Next video."

"But the guy's jizz falls right on the camera lens, man."

"That's exactly what I was afraid of," Buddy said. "Next."

vii. touching & butterflies

Marion opened his eyes and thought about the whiskey and the beer that had sent him to bed, about the way his tongue was sticking to the roof of his mouth, and how he wasn't generating any saliva. He thought about how his head was pounding.

He thought about water and aspirin and orange juice and toast and coffee and more water.

He was already looking forward to a long nap.

He shuffled along to the bathroom for a morning piss and drank some water from the faucet before returning to the bedroom. He pulled open the blinds to let in the daylight and saw his neighbor Dale on a ladder tending to one of his birdhouses, touching up Groucho Marx's mustache with black paint.

Chuck was out in his backyard, too, already drinking a beer and hosing off the canvas covering his nested climbing domes.

Marion looked down into his own yard. The night's wind had toppled his ashtray and there were cigarette butts strewn across the deck.

Then he saw it.

Something massive just beyond the deck taking up most of his lawn.

Sweat poured from his forehead. His heart raced. He pulled the shades, fearing the thing in the yard might see him. Though it didn't appear to have eyes.

Marion huddled in darkness, crying in his bedroom closet with the door shut, and he couldn't remember making the retreat. He was suddenly there, sweating and shivering in his boxer shorts, sitting on top of clothes and shoes he hadn't worn in years, surrounded by old wrinkled magazines and boxes filled with things he no longer needed. The clothes rocking on the hangers above brushed against his head and bare shoulders like taunting wraiths in a fairytale forest.

Marion couldn't shake from his head the image of the thing in his yard. He knew it couldn't be real.

I'm just hallucinating, he told himself. But this thought was of little comfort to him. *Only the insane hallucinate.*

Or the drugged.

Maybe it was the pot. He'd lay off the weed for a while. *Maybe Buddy got a batch sprinkled with PCP or some shit.*

Then he remembered that Buddy grew his own, and he knew Buddy wouldn't lace his stuff.

Food poisoning?

It took him a minute to remember what he'd eaten the night before: a couple of grilled hot dogs, some macaroni and cheese, potato chips. Nothing out of the ordinary. And he'd had an early dinner. If something he'd eaten was the cause, he figured he would have felt the effects before he even went to bed.

He thought back to what he'd seen through his window. Dale was up on a ladder and could have easily seen the thing in Marion's backyard. Chuck was outside and he, too, would have been able to see the thing. If it were real.

It wasn't.

He'd been hallucinating.

He was insane.

Temporary insanity, Marion hoped. *Maybe if I have another look through the bedroom window, the thing will be gone.*

Then he could go on with his life. He could get some water and aspirin and orange juice and toast and coffee and more water.

And maybe see a shrink.

But he'd have to look through the fucking

window first, and he didn't want to do that.

Marion huddled in the closet a while longer. The sweat drying on his skin made him itchy. He was cold and thought about turning up the heat. He decided he'd do that, get dressed, and look out the window again. He wanted a sense of normalcy before he had to face the thing in his backyard.

Because he just knew it hadn't gone away. It would be there, waiting for him.

He crawled out of the closet and stood, holding onto a wall to keep his shaking knees steady. He went out to the hall, fiddled with the environmental control unit—he never could remember how to override the programming—and managed to ratchet up the temperature a few degrees.

He returned to his bedroom, pulled on a sweatshirt, yesterday's pants, and some fresh socks.

He felt better now, sitting on the bed, fully dressed, almost normal. He was still hung-over, of course, but that was how normal felt lately.

He didn't go to the window for a second look. Instead, he went downstairs and brewed some coffee and slipped some stale bread into the toaster. He gulped down three glasses of water and two glasses of orange juice and sat down in his recliner and sipped the coffee.

The toaster popped, and he ate his toast and finished his coffee, doing everything he could to avoid the windows that looked out onto his backyard. He tried to think about anything other than the thing that may or may not be waiting for him outside.

He thought about work, which was something he usually tried not to do on the weekends. He thought about the unpaid bills, the house repairs he'd been putting off, thought about putting the house on the market and moving away.

Far away.

Then his craving for nicotine took over.

He slipped on a light jacket and pulled a knit cap down over his pillow-sculpted hair, something he wouldn't have done if he'd stepped out back. He usually didn't smoke on his front porch. It seemed less private somehow, although he was just as visible to his neighbors when standing at the back of his house.

He smoked his cigarette and thought about how fences only created the illusion of privacy. People just pretended they couldn't be seen in their backyards, while their neighbors pretended not to see them.

But no neighbor could politely unsee the thing he'd seen in his backyard. Dale and Chuck had been outside, going about their usual business, and this thing was massive. They couldn't have *not* seen it.

Yet, his neighbors weren't screaming. Marion didn't hear any approaching sirens.

The thing couldn't be there.

You're just hallucinating.

Only crazy. That's all.

He cursed and threw down his cigarette butt, watched it burn in the grass, the smoke trailing from it. He stared at it hard, willing it to burn forever because he'd just told himself that he'd have to go out back and investigate once the cherry died.

And it did, eventually. Marion looked longingly on the last tendrils of smoke as they vanished in the air.

He took a deep breath, exhaled through his nose, and stepped back inside. The house felt too warm now. His cheeks burned. He walked to the back of the house and paused before the sliding doors that opened onto the deck. The blinds were pulled across the view and twisted shut to keep out the light. He stood alone in his kitchen, shaking his head, laughing nervously to himself, unconsciously lighting up another cigarette.

He took a few drags before opening the blinds and pulling aside the sliding glass door to reveal that the giant mass of blue-veined flesh was still there. It dominated the view, rising up to a height equal to the deck's top railing. It was dimpled and pock-marked, discolored and sweaty. Patches of fine brown hair, wispy as down, could be seen along its edges, iridescent in the morning light.

Marion didn't see any orifices from where he stood, no sensory organs, no appendages.

It was just an enormous, useless mound of

flesh.

Marion stepped out onto the deck and left the door opened behind him.

Dale was still on his ladder. He'd moved it a few yards down the fence line and was hanging cheap costume jewelry around the neck of his Elvis birdhouse.

Chuck was sitting in a rocker on his back porch, drinking a beer, listening to some low-fi bluegrass recording on an antique portable cassette player.

Marion crossed the deck and went down the stairs to the small concrete patio below. He made sure to stay as far away from the mound as possible as he did so. He stood and smoked his cigarette and pretended to stare out into his backyard thoughtfully, but he was really examining the thing he now believed his mind had constructed.

He still saw no openings in the immense, alien thing, no proboscis, no closed eyelids. He did get the vague sense that it was breathing somehow. Although the movement was barely discernible, the flesh did expand and retract, rhythmically, as if it were sleeping.

How could a thing breathe without any holes?

He thought perhaps the movement he detected was the result of blood pulsing through the thing's veins. *The heart at its center must be massive and strong to be able to circulate blood through its giant body.*

Marion was surprised that he couldn't hear the beating muscle.

He rolled his eyes and pressed out his cigarette in an ashtray, chastising himself for speculating on the internal physical anatomy of an hallucination.

He then decided to conduct a sanity test. He picked up a broom and began sweeping the patio. The dried leaves flew off to collide with the mound, but they disappeared into its flesh instead.

He stopped sweeping.

The thing didn't open to admit the leaves; they just phased through its flesh, passed straight through with zero resistance.

Marion stepped cautiously to the end of the patio. The mound was only a few feet away from its edge. He started sweeping again, and this time he tried to touch the thing with the broom's bristles.

The end of the broom swept through the flesh again and again, and Marion felt no impact. It passed right through like the dead leaves had done a moment before. He was reminded of apparitions in old horror shows, of holographic projections in classic sci-fi films. The thing had no substance. It was just a harmless illusion.

Marion leaned the broom against the deck and stepped off the patio onto the back lawn. He reached out to lightly tap the mound with the tip of his shoe and was shocked to feel the thing make contact with the skin of his big toe.

The mound jiggled with the impact.

Marion fell backwards into the grass.

His shoe and sock had phased right through the thing and he'd felt its flesh.

And the mound had felt his.

This first contact made Marion nauseous. The thing was burning hot, feverish. The brief touch had been surprising, electrical. He had trouble catching his breath.

He twisted around and looked up, expecting to find Dale on his ladder staring down at him with concern and confusion on his face. But Dale wasn't there. Only the ladder leaned against the fence.

Relieved, Marion turned back around to face the mound. His hands were cold and the thing seemed to be producing real heat. He could feel it coming off the thing in waves, with each barely-discernible pulse of its flesh. He sat forward and could feel his cheeks warming. He shifted to his knees and held his hands out as if he were warming them near a blazing bonfire. He leaned in close and pressed his hands against the thing's skin. It was so warm, so good, so much like human flesh. He ran his hands over its surface, kneaded with his thumbs, and its veins disappeared and refilled with blue. He let his fingertips play lightly over its soft patches of hair. He squeezed.

The flesh was firm and elastic.

His stomach grumbled, and somehow he knew that the foodstuff he craved was inside the mound.

He felt himself stiffen, his pants straining against his groin, and knew that the release he needed was inside the mound.

And Marion soon discovered that these desires weren't a temporary result of his contact with its flesh. Even after he removed his hands from the thing, long after, as he did his best to go about the usual business of his day, he still thought about eating and fucking the mass of flesh in his backyard.

It was hard for him to think of anything else. Thoughts of the thing no longer sickened him, not after that very first touch. Instead, they brought on overwhelming sensations of covetous desire. His insides felt strange, filled with a nervous excitement that wouldn't go away.

It had been a long time since he'd felt this way and, as Marion sat on the bus, returning to work the next day, he recognized what he'd been feeling; the delightful torments of newfound love.

viii. head over heels

Marion only responded to urgent e-mails and answered the phone when he felt it was absolutely necessary. It was the day after he'd discovered the hill of flesh in his backyard, and he couldn't stop thinking about it. He couldn't wait to get home and be near it. The fact that his reaction to the thing had so suddenly turned from revulsion to carnal obsession didn't even register in his mind. He wanted nothing more than to feel its warmth again, to experience it completely. Upon touching it, the thing had transformed from a horrible curse into a mysterious gift. He wanted to open it and find out what was inside.

No, he needed to.

He left work two hours early without alerting anyone that he was doing so. He took a cab because he didn't feel like waiting on the bus.

As he listened to the sliding steel guitars blasting from the taxi's speakers, nearly choking on the overwhelming mint smell of the driver's dip, he had the terrible feeling that when he returned to his home, the thing would be gone. He silently urged the driver to run every red light and stop sign. But the driver wasn't telepathic and followed all the rules, spitting brown tobacco juice through his open window at every stop.

Marion tipped the driver and exited the cab, and it took everything he had to stop himself from running to the back of his house to check on the mound. He forced himself to follow his normal routine. He emptied his mailbox and walked up to his front door. The key wouldn't slip easily into the lock because his hands were shaking.

When he finally made it inside, he threw his mail on the kitchen table unexamined and pulled open the blinds onto the backyard.

It was still there.

He wiped his eyes on his shirt sleeves and barely acknowledged the tears, slid open the glass door and rushed to the edge of the deck to be close to the thing. He reached his hand over the top rail to touch it, then pulled back.

It was still light outside. Anyone, his neighbors, random passersby, might see him caressing some invisible beast. He knew he wasn't crazy now—the thing was real and magnificent—but he didn't want anyone to think he was.

He ran his fingers through his hair. He wanted so badly to touch the thing, to feel its flesh pressed against his own.

He lit up a cigarette and walked down the steps into the yard, stood before the mound and watched its subtle pulsing for the length of his smoke. He threw the butt into the grass and took a few steps forward and pressed his shins into its side. The cloth of his pants phased through it, and he instantly felt the charge of its overheated flesh against the skin of his legs. He couldn't believe how instantly and insanely hungry and horny he felt. His stomach and genitals ached.

Tears ran down his cheeks and he wiped them away. He was so relieved that the thing was safe and that he was touching it again.

Marion smoked another cigarette, smiling to himself, his heart beating fast with the secret pleasure he was taking in plain sight. He felt the same voyeuristic adrenaline rush he'd felt as a kid watching the neighbor girl undress through her bedroom window.

He finished his smoke and stepped back. The separation was almost painful. He was cold and shivering, much too cold for the moderate autumn weather. But he couldn't stand there like that all evening. He'd have to come back later, after dark, and visit when his actions wouldn't be so exposed.

He'd take a nap, set his alarm for midnight, and come back out while the neighborhood slept.

He went inside and found a bottle of Scotch, filled a glass with ice, and returned to the deck. He moved the table and a chair closer to the mound, sat down, and decided that he'd drink himself to sleep. He was too wired to sleep without an aid.

He sipped his Scotch, and the sky darkened. It was a beautiful sunset, a dozen shades of deep flickering orange and blazing yellows, as if the sun's rays were setting the horizon on fire.

He pulled one of Buddy's 'outside' joints from his cigarette pack, lit up, and meditated on the mound's contours and textures, all the tiny imperfections that somehow made it seem perfect. The pot was quick to kick in, and his mind's eye traveled inside the mound. He saw dozens of lithe bodies lying in wait, a variety of nude forms—not quite human, but unmistakably female, with semi-transparent wings folded at their backs—nestled in the mound's viscera, holding fleshy feeding tubes to their lips, drinking in the sustenance the mass womb produced for them, safe and content until it was time for them to be born into the world.

Marion imagined the mound's flesh unzipping and a vulva forming on its surface. He saw the creatures struggle free, one by one, and hover in the air above the deck, wings flapping, splashing him with the thing's juices. The winged creatures flew down to meet him, to undress him, to introduce him to their otherworldly pleasures.

Marion's eyelids were half closed as his unfettered mind created the feeling of a dozen mouths moving over his skin, kissing and sucking. He didn't want it to stop.

But the joint flared and a burning ash fell into his lap.

He jerked forward, brushed off his pants, and the ash burned itself out at his feet. He was completely out of his soft-core fantasy now and back to the hard reality of his wrought iron deck chair. It was full dark and the world was a much colder place. He dropped the joint into his ashtray, poured himself another drink, and started another cigarette.

He watched the mound for nearly two hours, drank Scotch well past the time the ice had melted, and went through half a dozen smokes before he decided it was time to go to bed.

He didn't realize how drunk he was until he tried setting his alarm. It took him several attempts to get it right, his slow reaction time causing him to skip 12 AM again and again. But he finally managed it and fell back onto his mattress fully dressed, with the lights on, and passed out.

Three hours later, his alarm clock woke him.

He hit the snooze button, sat up in bed, and ran his hands down his face, played with the hair on the back of his neck. Although his mouth was dry, he wasn't thinking about water.

He turned to the window overlooking the backyard. The shades were up, but he couldn't see outside. The three-way bulb in the bedside lamp was cranked up to its highest setting, so he found himself looking into a darkened mirror. Reflected back at him was a little man sitting alone in a large bedroom.

His hair was wild from the nap. He tried to smooth it with his palms, but it just wouldn't stay down. And he soon gave up trying to make it right.

He wanted to be outside.

He switched off his bedroom light and every light in every room in the house on his way out, making doubly sure to disable the lamp overlooking the backyard, the one with the erratic motion sensor, before stepping out onto the deck.

The moon was generous and Marion was disappointed. He didn't want to be seen.

The mound was pale silver in the moonlight, and the heat rising from its flesh fogged the air surrounding it. The thing seemed out of place in the darkness, like it didn't know how to properly reflect so little light. It looked like an image from a photo-realistic painting grafted onto a photograph. Like something that *almost* belonged.

Marion walked down into the grass and sat with his legs crossed before the mass of flesh and reached out both hands to touch it. The heat transferred to his palms was electric. His body shuddered and his stomach and groin ached. He moved his fingers over the thing's surface, pressed in with his thumbs, and wished for longer, sharper fingernails. He knew that he'd be able to tear into if they were longer. He decided not to trim them for a few weeks. He had to see, feel what was inside.

He sat there for some time, cross-legged, hands outstretched before him, looking to anyone who might be observing him like a man in a deep meditative state. He didn't care how crazy he might seem to his neighbors now, like some mad yogi of the darkness. He didn't care about anything beyond the flesh.

The ground numbed his legs, and it took a minor feat of willpower to take his hands off the thing's skin. He stood and stretched his legs, tried to rub feeling and warmth back into them. Then he mounted the steps and returned to the deck. He stood by the railing, leaned over and touched the top of the mound. He needed to drape himself over it.

Carefully, he climbed up onto the deck's railing and crouched there for a moment, looking in every direction to see if anyone was watching. He didn't see anyone, not a single light in a single window in a single neighboring house. And, feeling fairly confident that he wouldn't be seen, he jumped.

He landed face down and felt his clothes disappear beneath him, felt his flesh laid bare against that of the mound. It was wonderful. He closed his eyes and let out a gasping breath. The burning heat against his genitals was extraordinarily pleasurable. He started to move, in an attempt to produce friction, to bring himself to climax, but he found himself sliding down the far side of the mound headfirst.

He slipped too fast to get a firm grip on the flesh to stop himself.

His hands hit the ground and he tumbled off into the grass in a clumsy somersault. A hard landing on his back knocked the breath out of him. Two lonely stars, blurry through the tears welling in his eyes, winked at him from the sky above. The moon now seemed to glow even brighter, a spotlight shining down on his private shame.

Once the pain subsided, he crawled over next to the mound, curled himself around its base, and cursed himself for not doing this in the first place.

I'll sleep here tonight, and the neighborhood can just think I'm passed out drunk in the backyard.

He didn't want to be alone.

ix. an inflatable tent

The tent Marion wanted was out of stock when he'd ordered it online. It took nearly three weeks to arrive. When he shuffled up his driveway after yet another unproductive day at the office and saw the box on his front porch, he was elated. His pace quickened, and he snatched his package and hurried inside.

He searched frantically through the drawers in his kitchen for the box cutter. Of course, it was pushed way back in the last drawer he searched. He unsheathed the blade and, carefully, hands shaking with anticipation, sliced through the cardboard, removed the rolled-up tent and the foot pump, and rushed outside.

He took the steps down to the concrete patio two at a time, stripped the clear plastic wrapping from the bundle, and let it blow away in the breeze without a second thought. He unfolded the tent and laid it out flat on the lawn. He inserted the bellows into one of the inflatable support beams and pumped it with his foot.

As advertised, it only took twenty minutes to erect the three-person tent.

He felt light-headed when he was finished and sat down on the patio to rest. He admired his handiwork and lit up a smoke.

He threw the cigarette, half-smoked and still burning, into the yard and tested the tent's integrity. It seemed incredibly sturdy for something supported with air. Satisfied, he pushed the tent over the grass until nearly half its length disappeared into the mound's flesh. He then unzipped the opposite end of the tent and crawled inside.

Marion laughed to himself when he saw it, the mound presented to him in this private setting, its flesh phased through the wall of the tent, faintly pulsing and ready. He now had exactly what he wanted, unlimited, unseen access to its flesh.

He zipped closed the flaps behind him and crawled over to touch his secret pleasure. He dug into it with his overgrown fingernails and sliced a neat line in its flesh. An orange fluid seeped from the cut and dribbled down its side. He slid the index and middle fingers of his right hand inside the hole and touched its warm innards.

His eyes squinted shut with the immense pleasure of it. He stroked what felt like warm muscle and thrumming organs and longed to be inside of it.

He quickly unbuckled his belt and pulled off his pants. He looked down at himself and couldn't remember ever looking bigger or feeling harder in his life. He pressed himself inside the slit he'd opened and sighed when he felt the mound tighten around him, slowly, delicately, massaging the length of him.

He fell forward and buried his face in the warm flesh and began thrusting. He tried to pull free, wanting to re-live the experience of entering it for the first time, but the thing wouldn't let him go until he'd finished.

When he came, it felt like a mouth or a valve inside was sucking at the tip, drinking in every last drop. His climax flashed glowing green spider webs behind his eyelids. The world disappeared, dropped away. He felt like he was plunging down the hill of a roller coaster in total darkness.

The next thing he felt was cold. He opened his eyes and found himself curled up in a ball, naked and shivering. His legs were splattered with chilled semen and orange viscous fluids. He mopped himself with his undershirt and got dressed.

The hole he'd just fucked was still open and

dripping, and the bulb of some alien organ poked out. He crawled over and touched the thing. It was burning hot, and steam was rising off of it. It smelled delicious, and he reached out and tore it free.

More orange fluid oozed from the hole as the organ was ripped from its interstitial tissue.

Marion shoved his prize into his mouth and chewed, finishing it off in three greedy mouthfuls. It tasted even better than it smelled, and the warmth of it filled his belly, his entire body.

He'd never felt better in his life.

x. eaters

Buddy stood ankle-deep in the snow outside Trevor's window. He knocked for the third time and it opened. Trevor's head popped out. Steam billowed from his nostrils.

"Why the hell won't you use the door?" Trevor asked.

"I hate that fucking buzzer."

On Buddy's second trip to Trevor's place it had taken him twenty minutes to get past the buzzer. He swore he'd never go through that again. He'd been rapping on Trevor's window ever since.

Buddy suspected that Trevor had been playing with him, and had intentionally not let him in, timing the buzzes just right. It was something about the way he'd laughed throughout the whole ordeal.

Trevor was laughing that way now, and Buddy didn't like it.

"Come on in," Trevor said. "And leave your goddamned boots outside."

Buddy crawled in through the window and shook his boots off, let them drop into the snow, before pulling his stocking feet in behind him.

He brushed some crumbs off the deck chair next to Trevor's beanbag and had a seat. The kid's plastic table still sat between them, only now a handheld mirror, like something from a woman's vanity, lay on top of it. Four finely chopped lines of coke, a razor blade, and two rolled up dollar bills were reflected in the mirror's surface.

"You left the window open," Trevor said. "And you're still wearing that ridiculous coat."

"This ridiculous coat keeps me warm."

Trevor had told him repeatedly that his coat looked like something a five-year old boy might wear at the sled hill. Its puffy surface looked like stacked motocross tire inner tubes.

Buddy stood, removed his coat, and closed the window.

"I'm going to get something to drink," Buddy said. "You want anything?"

"There's a six pack of Old Carson in the fridge. Grab the whole thing and bring it in here."

Buddy did just that and returned to his seat. Two lines of coke were missing from the mirror.

"Here." Trevor sniffled, sliding the mirror across the table in Buddy's direction. "Let's get to it."

Buddy wasn't a fan of the cocaine. He only did it when someone was offering it up. He'd never bought the stuff and couldn't see himself ever getting into the habit. He hated having a cold, and that was what it was like for Buddy—intentionally inducing cold symptoms for not much of a pleasurable payoff. He never felt the elation that others reported, the racing thoughts, the energy, the sense of invincibility. He felt none of that. Instead, he always felt as if his brain had stopped working, like everything he heard or saw passed straight through unprocessed. He never felt elated, just the somewhat disturbing sensation of his teeth grinding together. And instead of feeling invincible, he'd become immobile, like his arms and legs were in a constant state of anticipation, waiting for a special signal that his brain was incapable of delivering.

But, despite all of that, Buddy never turned the stuff down when it was offered. He took the rolled-up bill and snorted the lines. It was rude to refuse such an expensive offering.

Buddy sniffled and swallowed, and a few minutes later, he had a sour stomach.

He'd forgotten about the sour stomach.

He opened a beer and finished it off in a few gulps to offset the unease in his gut. He opened another, took a few sips, and started rolling a joint.

Every time he did coke, he tried to neutralize its effects by drinking too much and smoking a lot of weed. This never worked, and he knew it never worked, but he did it anyway. And the end result was that the coke prevented him from realizing he was drinking too much, and he smoked through a bunch of his weed for no good reason.

And he always woke up the next morning feeling horrible.

Trevor cut up and snorted another line.

Buddy licked and sealed his joint and set it on fire. He took a drag and asked, "What have you got for me tonight? Hopefully something else, like the sorority nun thing."

The last time he'd stopped over, Trevor had played a video he'd shot through a dirty window at a sorority house in Wisconsin. Some sort of hazing was going on. The pledges were stripped down, lined up on hands and knees along a far wall while their elder sisters, wearing cheap Halloween costume nun's habits and nothing else, whipped them with sopping wet rags. Trevor had told him that the rags were soaked with vodka.

"If you want more naked nun videos, buy a computer and learn how to use the Internet." Trevor flipped open his laptop and the plasma screen hanging on the wall flashed on. "I've got some serious craziness to show you tonight. I'll be leaving town in about a week, and you'll probably want to leave, too, after you see this."

Buddy laughed. Trevor was getting dramatic again. He was the same way before he showed the gunshot suicide video he'd captured in Portland. Buddy had not pissed his pants when he saw that as Trevor had promised he would. He just felt dirty afterward, and had trouble shaking the image of the blood gushing out of the man's nose and mouth. It still haunted him every night when he went to sleep. The man had just popped himself like he was a water balloon. He didn't think he'd ever shake the look of surprise and disbelief in the man's eyes.

Trevor double-clicked and an image expanded to fill the screen. It was an aerial view of a suburban neighborhood.

"Exciting stuff." Buddy blew smoke through his nostrils.

Trevor ignored this comment and said, "This is from out in California. Take a good look."

"What am I looking for exactly?"

"Just try to capture what you're seeing, OK?" Trevor paused for a moment. "Got it?"

"I guess."

"OK," Trevor closed the file and opened another aerial photograph of a suburban neighborhood. "Now have a look at this."

"What? Another suburb. I'm not getting it."

"It's the same place. This picture was taken just six months later."

"OK. I'm still not getting it."

Trevor sighed, pulled up the first file, and

re-sized the windows so that they could look at the images side-by-side. "See it now?"

Buddy took a swig of beer and sat forward. He did see it. "Yeah. What are all those things in their backyards?"

"Sheds mostly."

"So, what you're trying to show me is that some retailer in California had a great deal on sheds?"

"No. Be patient." Trevor closed out of the images and scrolled through a file tree until he found what he was looking for. "You'll probably recognize this picture." He double-clicked, and the screen showed another aerial photograph. This one was obviously scraped from a television newscast. The station's call letters were at the top left of the screen, and the scrolling news ticker at the bottom was blurred and frozen in time.

"Shit." Buddy took in the sprawling devastation. He'd not seen or heard anything about it since it first happened five years before. "Shit, yeah. I remember. This was all over the news for weeks."

"Yeah. And then you didn't hear anything about it at all. The story was just dropped. Total blackout. This is the best picture I can find of the Hanover Block. Clean photos are nearly impossible to get a hold of. Although, I'm sure thousands were taken at the time."

"The Hanover Block. Shit, I almost completely forgot about it."

"I'm sure that's somebody's intent. That we do forget about it."

"OK, thanks for reminding me. I feel horrible and depressed. Why the hell are you showing me this?"

"It's the same neighborhood. Before and after, Buddy."

"And? I'm obviously missing something. I'm high, but not that high."

"I know. Give me some time here. Look." Trevor re-opened the image of the Hanover Block with all the new sheds in the backyards. "This up-cropping of backyard construction is a symptom of a kind of infection that swept through their neighborhood."

"What kind of infection causes people to buy sheds for their backyards?"

"Remember those levitation videos you seemed to like so much?"

"Yeah, they were really special."

"All of those people were infected."

"Let me guess. You took all of that footage on the Hanover Block before it went boom. You just happened to be living there and caught onto what was really going on and got out just in time."

"Yes and no. I did live a few blocks away, and I did shoot some video there. But most of the levitation videos I shot were shot elsewhere. This shit is spreading across the country."

"What shit?"

"I'll show you." Trevor replayed the video

of the guy suspended in the air, thrusting his pelvis down toward the hidden camera. "Remember this guy?"

"Oh, yeah. I was going to ask you to play that one for me again. Thanks."

"Well, this isn't special effects, man. None of the so-called levitation videos are faked. This guy is actually on top of an object only he can see and touch."

"OK, I'm pretty sure you're insane or just fucking with me here. But I'll ask anyway, just to humor you. What sort of object?"

"Since it's something only he can see and touch, I can only show you an artist's rendering. And it's pretty crude."

Trevor closed out of the floating humping man video and the aerial photos and opened what looked like a scanned drawing done with a failing ballpoint pen. It appeared to be the work of a talented eight-year old kid. There were trees and bushes and a privacy fence in the background. In the foreground—under a smattering of scribbled letter Vs that represented birds in flight and a smiley-face sun, and next to a slide and a swing set—there was a large hill. All of the artist's time had been spent on the hill's details. Everything else in the picture was obviously an afterthought, sketched in hastily to provide context.

"I don't think I'm seeing what you want me to see here," Buddy said.

"Look right at the center of the drawing."

"The hill?"

"Look closer. Here." Trevor's mouse pointer turned into a magnifying glass, and he rolled the scroll-wheel on his mouse to zoom in on the hill. "That's not grass, Buddy."

Buddy squinted. "What is it then?"

"Hair. And you see all those crazy looking letter Ys?"

"Yeah."

"Those are supposed to be veins."

"Veins?"

"Yeah. It's a mound of living flesh."

"How can you know that?"

"I've managed to find a few Usenet groups, where some of these hilljackers have gotten together to share their experiences. That's what these infected people are seeing. These mounds were all over the Hanover Block."

"Wait a second. Hilljackers?"

"Yeah, that's what they call themselves. Hilljackers. Mound pounders."

"Why?"

"Think about it."

Buddy thought about it. He whistled through his teeth. "It seems like this shit would be all over the Internet. Something like this would proliferate."

"Unless everyone involved feels it's in everyone's best interest to not let this thing go viral. I only managed to find a couple hilljacker blogs. But this stuff doesn't stay up long. Nobody wants a repeat of Hanover. So, either the hilljackers take the stuff down themselves, or the agency that polices this stuff has it killed, because they don't know how this infection spreads. It could spread by word-of-mouth, for all they know."

"What government agency hunts down giant mounds of flesh?"

"The DTTF. The Domestic Threats Task Force. It's a subset of Homeland Security. They mainly spend their time sabotaging the formation of labor unions. They're the ones who blew the Hanover Block to hell. The gas main explosion story is total bullshit."

"How the hell can you know all this shit?"

"I know how to use a computer. I was busting through my dad's parental control software when I was ten years old."

"OK. Why does some government agency give a shit if a bunch of crazies are fucking imaginary mounds of flesh in their backyards?"

"They're not crazy. And the mounds aren't imaginary. These things are absolutely real."

"But only to the people who can see them. They're nuts."

"No, I really don't think they are. The difference is that we can't watch a schizophrenic climb up on the shoulders of his invisible tormentor."

"So, these hilljackers can actually physically interact with their delusions. What's the harm?"

"They fuck and feed off these things compulsively. It becomes an obsession. Once they're hooked, they can no longer function in society."

"Fuck."

"Yeah. They scoop out handfuls of their innards and eat them. Usually after they finish fucking the things."

Buddy was quiet for a moment. "Yeah, that is pretty disgusting, isn't it?"

Trevor nodded. "It is. But that's not the worst of it. I'll show you."

The interior of a large tool shed flashed on the screen, large enough to comfortably accommodate a dining room table and one ornately carved wooden throne. An antique lantern hung above the table. Its fogged glass obscured the light bulb hidden inside.

"How the hell'd you get this shot?" Buddy asked. "It looks like you're just standing in there."

"Drilled a hole in the wood. Slipped in a camera with a pinhole lens and patched it up. It takes only about a minute and a half. This one took a bit longer because I needed to install some additional hardware, so that I could get lots of footage."

"You've got balls. Jesus, man."

"Shit, he didn't notice. The guy was pretty messed up. Just look at him."

The door to the shed swung inward and momentarily blocked the camera's view. The door closed and a man's face was revealed. The tip of his nose almost poked the camera lens, but Buddy saw a vulture lunging at his face, pecking at his eyes. When the man turned to latch and lock the door, Buddy saw that the grotesque avian shape of the man's nose wasn't an optical illusion created by the fish-eye lens. The man's beard was trimmed short and neat, all zagging lines and curves, like he must have used some sort of shaving stencil. His eyes were almost all pupil, the irises nearly black, the corneas just flickering white crescents.

He was wearing a dusty dinner jacket with tails, pinstriped pants, and a leather vest missing most of its buttons.

He didn't have a chin, and his lips were quivering as if with a barely constrained hysteria. He looked too thin, and filthy, like he hadn't had a bath in weeks. Unwashed hair curled up just above his ears and at the nape of his neck.

He carried a silver tray with a large silver serving dome at its center. He looked like a butler who had stuck with his family throughout their tragic riches-to-rags story. He placed the tray on the table and sat on the throne.

He lifted the silver cloche to reveal a decanter filled with brown liquid, a small bucket of ice, and a highball glass. He fixed himself a drink and lifted the glass for a toast, turned to his right, as if he were honoring the ghost of a long dead relative. He tilted it back and poured another. He took his time with the second drink, eyes fixed on the unseen subject of his toast.

He used both hands, pressed against the table, to push himself out of the throne's plush cushions. He then began to slowly undress, methodically draping his discarded clothing over the back of the throne. The man's arms and legs were thin and flabby. He had a slight paunch. His naked flesh mottled and unhealthy. His penis small and twisted, fully erect.

Buddy was thankful that the freakish little thing was only turned toward the camera for a second.

The man turned away and did something with his hands that was blocked by the position of his body. And a moment later, he thrust his hips. His hands became visible again, and they seemed to be pressed up against some unseen object supporting his weight.

"OK," Buddy said. "I get it. He's put up a shed to hide his sessions with his little flesh hill. And since it can only be touched by him, its flesh passes right through the walls. Now, do we have to sit here and watch this guy fucking away? Can we turn it off now?"

"No, we can't. But I'll fast-forward it."

Watching the man bucking in sped-up, jerky motions didn't make it any better. But it only took a few seconds for the guy to reach his climax and collapse, exhausted, against the invisible mound.

"All right. Look at this." Trevor paused the

video, the man was now suspended in the air, curled up in a fetal position, a few feet above the wooden floor of the shed. It looked like he was sucking his thumb. "He's crawled inside the thing."

"Shit."

"I know. And he never comes out."

"What do you mean?"

"I'll show you."

The screen went black except for a sliding control bar across the bottom. Trevor scooted the arrow-shaped slider to the right with his mouse pointer. "This is a few days later."

The man was in the same position. His skin had grown gray and bloated. There was a puddle of piss and shit on the floor below him.

The screen went black.

"Now, this is about two weeks later," Trevor said.

The shed's interior returned. The man's body was still suspended in the same position, but it was now wilted and black, like it had been drained of all moisture.

Buddy could see the man's vertebrae, every one in great detail, poking through the paper-thin skin on his back.

The shed door burst open, startling Buddy. When the door closed again, a police officer was standing there, accompanied by a man and a woman in suits and long winter jackets.

Trevor jumped ahead in the video again.

Two men in hazmat suits pulled the man

out of the air. He came apart in crisp chunks. They sealed his remains in a black plastic bag. They swept the floor of the little pieces that had flaked away when they pulled him apart and poured them into the black bag before zipping it up.

The screen went black again and Buddy and Trevor sat together in silence for quite some time.

Buddy was scared. He twisted open another beer and gulped it down. Trevor cut himself another line and snorted it up his nose.

"Are you ready for part two?" asked Trevor, smiling, white powder circling the rims of both nostrils.

Buddy didn't answer. He kept staring at the black screen. He was still seeing the man's body being pulled apart, like a sculpture made from thousands of tightly compacted autumn leaves.

"I'll interpret your silence as a 'yes,'" Trevor said. A list of files appeared on the screen, and he tapped his keyboard a few times and the screen showed another aerial photograph of a suburban neighborhood.

"Back to the Hanover Block?" Buddy asked. "I think I've had enough of that."

"No. This is your neighborhood, Buddy. This picture was taken about six months ago."

Buddy knew where this was headed.

Trevor opened another file, another aerial photograph. "And this is your neighborhood about two months ago."

Buddy knew exactly what to look for this

time. The backyards were now infested with sheds and other small buildings. He didn't know what to say, so he drank his beer, lit up another smoke.

"This is something I hadn't seen before," Trevor said, pointing to a black circle on the screen. "When I spotted this, I had to go out and see what it was. This is a geodesic climbing dome, two of them, actually, stacked on top of each other, with a black tarp thrown over it. This guy has probably opened dozens of little fuck holes in his mound. Hitting it from every angle."

"Where's that?" asked Buddy.

"Right next door to your pal Marion's place." Trevor cleared his throat, took a swig of beer. "I heard about what happened to his wife and kid."

"Yeah. That was pretty fucked up. He still won't drive a car. He'll take a cab sometimes, but always sits in the back seat, behind the driver."

"Shit. It's been five years, hasn't it?"

"More like seven." Buddy produced a plastic baggie and began crumbling up weed to make another joint. "So, what are you going to do with all of this?"

"What do you mean?"

"It looks like you've got enough here to prove something really messed up is really going on." Buddy wet the glue on the edge of the rolling paper with his tongue. "Are you going to expose the whole thing?"

"I don't know. Maybe. I really have thought

about it a lot lately. But I've got to figure out a way to do it without exposing myself. All of this evidence was gathered illegally. I don't really want to get locked up again. Or killed."

"The DTTF?" Buddy asked, handing over the smoking joint.

"Them or the hilljackers." Trevor took a drag and exhaled. "They're fiercely protective of their backyard fuck buddies. And the eaters are particularly defensive, from what I understand."

"Eaters?"

"Yeah, I guess some people don't fuck their mounds. They just feed off them."

xi. background voices

The phone was ringing again. He'd ignored it for the past two hours, had ignored it for days. If it was human resources, then they were giving him more chances than he deserved. He'd listened to their messages on his machine—one a day over the past week—transform from real concern to warnings, to veiled threats. Then finally, the day before, a message informed him that his employment was being terminated due to job abandonment.

He'd lost his job and didn't care. Marion hadn't cared then, when he heard the message. He had money in the bank, enough to keep him going until he solved the mystery of the thing in his backyard. He felt closer to solving that mystery as every new day passed. It wouldn't be long.

The phone kept ringing.

Why aren't they leaving a message?

Marion separated himself from the kitchen floor. He was half naked, wearing only an old pair of sweatpants. The skin on his bare back didn't want to release its hold on the vinyl flooring. It gave way reluctantly, with a tiny sucking noise. He'd been sleeping in the kitchen for weeks. He couldn't stand to be too far from the backyard. The kitchen was the only room in the house with two heating vents, and every night, after spending hours out in the cold with the mound, he'd stumble back inside and collapse on the floor right between them.

On this morning, he had no idea what had become of his shirt. His shoes and socks were missing, too. Usually, he woke up fully dressed, confused by his surroundings. Waking up next to the fridge continued to catch him by surprise.

Marion gripped the island at the center of the kitchen and pulled himself to his feet. He picked up the cordless phone and looked at the display. It was blank now; the phone had finally stopped ringing. He pressed the down arrow on the keypad and flipped through the last five missed calls. They were all from the same number, labeled as 'Cell Phone,' and all had come in within the last two hours. It wasn't human resources. It was a number he vaguely remembered. He tried—rubbing the bridge of his nose between thumb and index finger—but couldn't put a name to the number.

He placed the phone back in its cradle, and it immediately began ringing again. He checked the display. The same number. He took up the phone, pressed the 'Talk' button, put it to his ear and listened.

He heard only faint breathing on the other end, then a surprised sounding, "Hello?"

Marion tried to place the voice, but couldn't.

"Who is this?" he asked, and was startled by the sound of his own voice. Scratchy and foreign. He realized that he'd not spoken aloud, to himself or anyone else, for over a week.

Whoever was on the other end didn't answer.

"Hello?" Marion said. "Who is this?"

"Marion? Is that you?"

"Yes. Who's calling?"

"You sound different."

"I've got a cold." Marion lied. "Who am I speaking with?"

"It's Stew."

Stew Bennett. Marion hadn't spoken to Stew since right after the accident. Stew had a wife and two kids, two girls. He could hear their voices in the background, the girls, sounding much older now, arguing over a remote control.

Over the years, Marion had moments of regret about dumping his old high school friend. But he could never find the right time or the courage to make things right.

He felt shame now, holding the phone, saying nothing, thinking about all the Christmas cards he'd received from the Bennetts over the years, the ones he'd thrown away without opening, not wanting to see the photographs he could feel through the envelopes.

"Stew Bennett," said the voice. "Are you still there? Marion?"

Just barely.

He felt like screaming and dropping the phone and stomping it to pieces. But instead, he said, "Yeah. I'm here. Like I told you. Just not feeling well."

"I won't keep you," Stew said. "Did you watch the news last night?"

"No. I usually don't."

"Did you see the paper this morning?"

"I don't get the paper."

"OK. Hold on. Let me step into the other room."

Marion heard footsteps and a door clicking shut. The girls' voices were cut off.

"I don't know if you know this," Stew said, "but Trevor Cadwallader moved back into town."

"Yeah. Buddy told me. I guess he's here for a few months for a job."

Marion knew Stew still kept in contact with

Buddy. He'd seen his car parked down the block from Buddy's sometimes, and when he did, he just kept on walking.

Thinking of this made him feel guilty all over again. He wanted nothing more than to disconnect the call.

"Yeah," Marion said. "I wasn't particularly thrilled to hear the news. The guy's a creep."

"Yeah." The way Stew said this didn't give the impression that he agreed with Marion. Something in the way he said it made Marion feel very uncomfortable.

A thick silence fell between them. For a moment Marion thought that Stew may have accidentally hit the mute button on his phone. The faint breathing was gone.

"Marion," Stew said, "Trevor's apartment building burned down last night. Every tenant in the building is dead."

Marion didn't know what to say; he'd just called a guy who'd burned to death a creep. All he could manage was, "Shit."

"I know. It's pretty messed up. Buddy told me that Trevor was into some crazy stuff lately. The police are saying it's obviously a case of arson. Whoever did it wasn't trying real hard to hide it."

"Jesus. You think Trevor was the target?"

"It's certainly likely. Based on some of the stuff Buddy's been telling me."

"Does Buddy know?"

"I can't get a hold of him. He might have

been in the fire, for all I know. He was spending a lot of time over there. The police haven't released all the names yet."

"Shit."

"Yeah. And Buddy's not answering his phone."

"Buddy never answers his phone."

"You have a point. But he watches the news. Religiously. He'd be answering his phone this morning."

"Yeah. You'd think."

Another long silence. Then Marion found himself saying, "I'll walk over there and give you a call when I get back."

"Would you? I would have gone myself, but I'm watching the girls. Michelle's at her sister's today, for a baby shower."

"I'll call you when I get back."

Marion didn't say good-bye.

xii. log cabin in winter

Marion waited on Buddy's doorstep for a long time. He was still in his sweatpants and had pulled on a t-shirt and some socks. The winter coat and hiking boots did nothing to the keep the chill from his skin. He wasn't wearing a hat.

He banged on the door, not quite understanding why he bothered. Buddy's car wasn't in the driveway, and he never parked in the garage. It was too filled with junk.

He knew Buddy wasn't there.

He tried the knob, and it was unlocked.

Marion stepped inside, closing the door behind him, thinking he'd hear the sound of approaching sirens any minute.

"Buddy?" he called out, not expecting to hear an answer.

He walked up the stairs to Buddy's bedroom. It was empty, and the sheets were stripped from the mattress. The spare bedroom was empty, too, except for a few teetering shelves of old paperbacks.

Marion went downstairs into the living room. Buddy's television and stereo were both missing.

Marion peered through the window over the kitchen sink and saw the Tupperware containers from their breakfast picnic half-buried in snow. And just beyond these remnants, standing askew in the backyard, was a little molded plastic log cabin, a cheap playhouse built for preschoolers, something Marion imagined Buddy picking up at a garage sale for five bucks.

The padlock on the basement door was missing.

The smell of gasoline was overpowering.

Buddy's done a very bad thing and skipped town.

Marion went down the steps. The door to Buddy's grow room was torn off its hinges and lying on the cement floor.

The secret room was empty. The expensive lights and the plants were gone. Only a few leaves and seeds littered the floor.

Marion found a pair of gloves next to the

washer and drier. They were soaked through with gasoline. He dropped them immediately and ran up the stairs, through the house, and out the front door.

He stopped running as soon as he reached the porch and tried not to look suspicious. He looked around to see if anyone had seen him exit the house.

He didn't see anyone.

Relieved, he walked home like he was just out for a stroll. It seemed like every car slowed as it drove past, like every driver wanted to get a good look at him.

Marion hoped he was just imagining this. He didn't want to be noticed. He didn't want to get involved. He didn't want to talk to the police about what he'd seen at Buddy's house. He didn't want to talk to anyone about it.

When he unlocked his front door and walked into the musty warmth of his home, he decided that he wasn't going to call Stew back. He couldn't stand the thought of implicating Buddy, or hearing the girls laughing in the background.

He parted the blinds above the kitchen sink and looked outside at the mound waiting patiently for him. He needed its company now more than he'd ever needed it before. Needed its comfort. Needed its power to make him forget.

Marion walked out onto the deck, down the stairs, onto the patio. He stepped out into the white yard. His boots crunched in the snow. He brushed powder from the top of the tent.

Inside was like being at the aquarium, surrounded by waves of light and shadow. The wind ruffled the canvas, and he pictured himself trapped inside a jellyfish. He zipped the tent closed and undressed.

He crawled over and placed his hands next to the healed scar he'd opened night after night to take his pleasure. He used his fingernails to slice through the flesh, but didn't stop at re-opening the same wound. He kept digging until he'd opened a gash large enough to crawl through, and found himself staring into a whale's mouth turned sideways, its lips quivering impatiently.

Marion reached a hand inside. Steam rose all around him, blurring his vision. He pushed his arm in deeper, and soft organs moved aside. The mound's orange fluids, hot and sticky, coated his flesh.

Then he found what he was looking for, the thing he hadn't known was there until just a moment before. His hand closed around a slick tube, and he pulled.

It didn't resist him. It slipped out of the whale's mouth and Marion caught it with both hands.

The tube was covered with pulsing veins and dripped with strings of thick mucus. The end he held in his hands was open, and he could see the tube was hollow.

The smell that escaped was irresistible, and

he put the tube to his mouth and sucked. His belly filled with warmth.

Marion's eyes closed, and he crawled into the mound, the tube still in his mouth. He pulled his legs in behind him and tried to push himself deep into the steaming warmth of its internal organs.

His back pressed up against a cold membrane, and although he tried, he found that he could go no farther. Something about the barrier seemed foreign, like it didn't belong.

Then he realized it was the wall of the tent and stopped fighting it. He opened his eyes again and the whale's mouth closed, shutting out the light, and he never felt warmer in his life, never felt safer, so protected and content.

He gripped the tube with both hands, curled his legs around its length, and drank deeply. He found it wasn't hard to forget the world outside, and his sated mind held no regrets.

connect with the author online

blog: gregorxane.blogspot.com

goodreads: goodreads.com/GregorXane

booklikes: gregorxane.booklikes.com

twitter: twitter.com/GregorXane

e-mail: gregorxane@gmail.com

Made in the USA
Lexington, KY
10 September 2017